The Wacky Wedding

A BOOK OF ALPHABET ANTICS

Pamela Duncan Edwards

Illustrated by Henry Cole

HYPERION BOOKS FOR CHILDREN
NEW YORK

On each page of this book, the letter of the alphabet is hidden in the artwork. There is also an object beginning with that letter somewhere on the page.
Can you find them?

Printed in Singapore.

This book is set in 22-point Eldorado Roman.
The artwork for each picture was prepared using acrylic and colored pencil.

FIRST EDITION
3 5 7 9 10 8 6 4 2

Library of Congress Cataloging-in-Publication Data
Edwards, Pamela Duncan.
Wacky Wedding: [a book of alphabet antics]/Pamela Duncan Edwards; illustrated by Henry Cole.—1st ed.
p. cm.
Summary: An alphabetical ant wedding, attended by the other animals, is beset by various disasters.
ISBN 0-7868-0308-8 (hardcover). ISBN 0-7868-2248-1 (lib. bdg.)
[1. Weddings—Fiction. 2. Ants—Fiction. 3. Animals—Fiction. 4. Alphabet.]
I. Cole, Henry, 1955–ill. II. Title.
PZ7.E26365Wac 1999
[E]—dc21 98-47171

An army of ants attended a wedding,
once on an April afternoon.

Blossoms were held by the beautiful queen bride.
Butterfly bridesmaids were dresssed in bright blue.

Carpenter ants carried a cicada with confetti.
Cleaner ants carted the colony's cake.

"Dear me!" cried a dragonfly. "The daydreamers have dropped it!"

"Disgraceful!" declared a drone in disgust.

Eager earthworms helped reerect it.
"It's more elegant than earlier!" an earwig exclaimed.

Flying into the forest came the groom and his family, as a foolish fruit fly let some fruit fall.

"Good grief!" groaned a grackle as the groom
hit the ground.
"Get back!" gulped a grasshopper.
"He's gasping for air."

"Half-wit!" howled the Queen at the hysterical fruit fly.
A honeybee handed her his handkerchief.

In spite of his injuries, the bridegroom insisted
the inchworm must hold the wedding immediately.

"Jingle," rang bellflowers for the joyful occasion.
Jolly June beetles danced a jig.

Kicking her heels and skipping with glee, a katydid giggled, "Look, they're kissing."

Lounging on a leaf, a ladybug laughed.
"They've loved each other since they were larvae."

"Magnificent marriage," murmured a mole,
his head emerging from a mossy mound.

"Nice nuptials," announced a nearsighted nymph.
A nuthatch nodded and nuzzled his sweetheart.

On an oak leaf they formed an orderly line.
Oatmeal cookies and orangeade
were offered to all.

"Perfect," said the Queen, sparkling with pride.
She watched the pupae being powdered and pampered.
Then—what a panic! *Plipity-plop*.
The bride tripped into a puddle.

"Quick!" squealed the quails. "Quiet down!
Quit quivering and quaking and help the Queen."

Red fire ants rushed right to the rescue.
"Ready! Form a rope," they roared.

"See, she's sinking," sobbed a soldier ant,
for sadly the ant string was slightly too short.

Tearful treehoppers trembled on a twig.
"A terrible tragedy is taking place."

"Use my umbrella," a leaf-cutter ant urged.
"I understand she's unable to swim."

Valiantly a velvet ant cried, "I volunteer!
I vow my voyage shall not be in vain."

"Watch it wobbling," whispered a whirligig beetle,

as the wind whipped the watercraft over the waves.

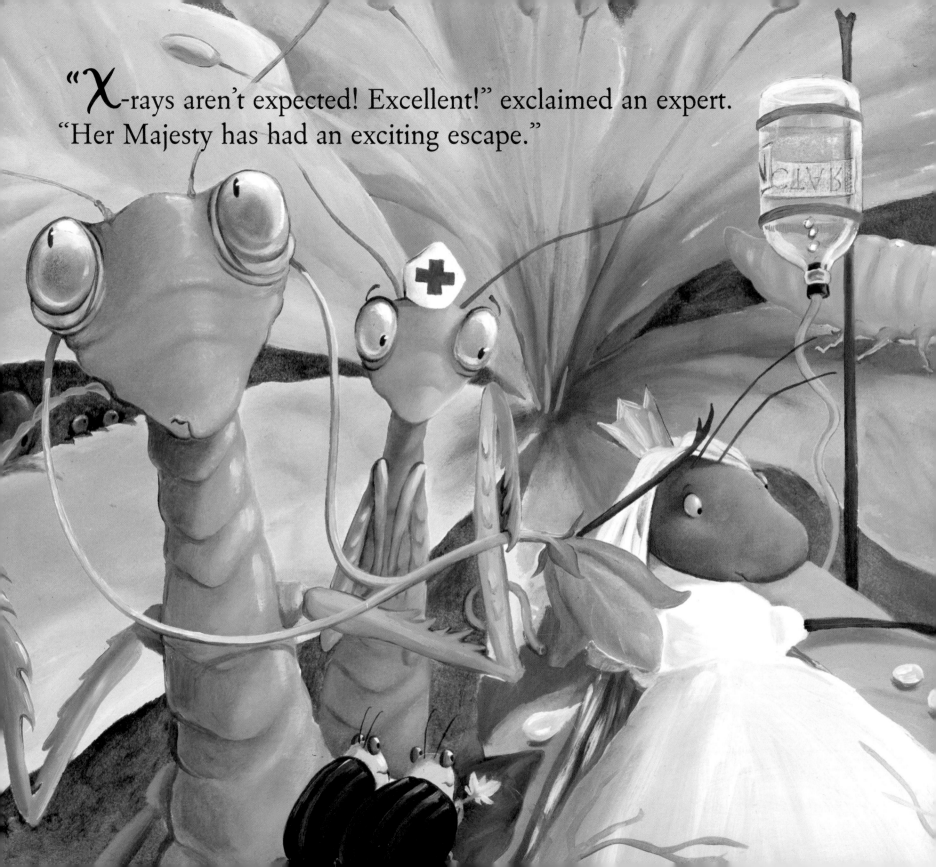

"X-rays aren't expected! Excellent!" exclaimed an expert.
"Her Majesty has had an exciting escape."

Yik-yakity went their voices.
Then tired youngsters started yelling, and
the yellow-jacket band went yawning off to bed.

Zebra swallowtails on their zithers strummed a lazy tune.
"May all your days be dazzling," buzzed a dozen bees.

Zillions of fireflies set ablaze the night sky
as drowsily the ants zigzagged home toward their nests.

I'm "Velvet Ant"! Not really an ant — just a close relative... a WASP!
GOSH! we cleaner ants had a tough time keeping the nest tidy this week
Soldier ants! Well done! Excellent job of guarding the Queen!
Just doing our duty, sir!
Hi! I'm a leaf-cutter ant! I came from Louisiana and brought my umbrella!
Welcome Fire Ants!
Love this spicy food!
It's almost as hot as my bite!